TATTERHOOD

by
ROBIN MULLER

Scholastic Canada Ltd.
123 Newkirk Road, Richmond Hill, Ontario, Canada

Canadian Cataloguing in Publication Data
Muller, Robin.
   Tatterhood

ISBN 0-590-71446-5

I. Title.

PS8576.U44T37 1984a   J398.2'7   C84-098562-2
PZ8.M84Ta 1984a

Design by Kathryn Cole

6 5 4 3   Printed in Hong Kong   2 3 4/9

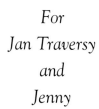

For
Jan Traversy
and
Jenny

They took the blossoms of the oak,
and the blossoms of the meadow-sweet,
and produced from them a maiden,
the fairest and most graceful
that man ever saw.
– from a fourteenth century
Welsh manuscript

Long ago and far away, a King and a Queen lived in a beautiful palace overlooking the sea. Green lawns, bright flowers and sparkling fountains spread around it. But for all its wonder, it was a lonely place, for the King and Queen had no children. To hide her despair, the Queen took long walks by herself in the country.

One spring day, the Queen came upon a little cottage that was almost hidden by a wood. Above the cottage door a dove had built her nest and was busily tending her young.

Feeling a terrible longing, the Queen sat down on a fallen tree and began to cry. Instantly a little old woman came out of the cottage to see what was the matter. "My lady, why do you weep?" she asked.

"I weep," said the Queen, "because I have everything except what I want most — children of my own."

Now, unknown to the Queen, the little old woman was a witch — but a good witch with a kind heart — and she felt very sorry for the Queen. "I can promise you a child," she said finally, "but you must do exactly as I say."

"Anything," cried the Queen, "so long as I can have a baby!"

So the witch told the Queen what to do. Before she went to bed that night, she was to take two pails of water and wash herself in both of them. Then she was to splash water from each of the pails under the bed.

"Come morning," said the witch, "two flowers will have grown under your bed. Eat the fair one, but the other you must not touch. No matter how great your desire," she warned, "you must not touch the ugly flower."

That night the Queen did as the witch had instructed her. After washing herself in the two pails, she splashed the water, then lay down and fell into a deep sleep.

The next morning, as soon as she awoke, the Queen threw back the covers and peered under the bed. True to the witch's promise, two flowers were growing there. One was soft gold with a purple centre, velvety as the sky between the stars. Shimmering patterns touched the petals with the colours of sunrise. The other flower was yellow as a lizard's eye. Its centre was black as a sorcerer's cauldron, and strange blotches marked the petals like angry purple bruises.

Without wasting a moment, the Queen plucked the beautiful flower and ate it. But so delectable was its blossom and so overpowering its scent that she was filled with a desperate craving for more. Before she could stop herself, she had snatched the other flower and eaten it even as she remembered the witch's terrible warning.

Within the year the Queen gave birth to a baby — a very strange baby girl. The child had matted black hair and a face like a little demon, and the moment she was born she started roaring, "Mama!" Before long she was racing through the palace on a baby goat, whooping and banging away with a long wooden spoon.

The Queen, after waiting so long for a baby, was horrified at the sight of her daughter. "If I am indeed your Mama," she cried, "God give me the strength to cope with you."

The baby looked at the Queen with glittering eyes. "Do not fear, dear Mother," she said, "for one will come after me who will delight your heart."

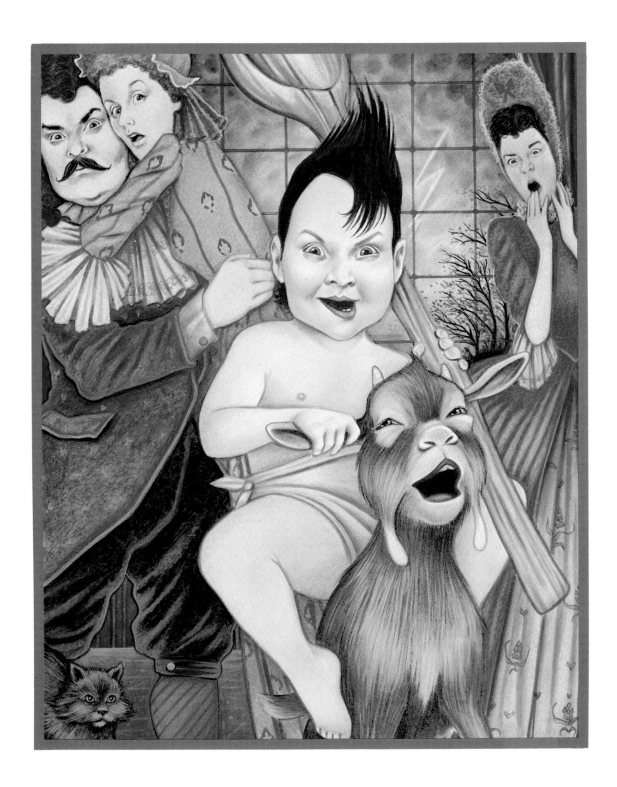

Sure enough, the next year the Queen had another baby — a girl who was good-natured and so fair that all who saw her said they had never beheld such beauty. The Queen loved the second baby beyond all telling and named her Belinda. Her elder daughter was called "Tatterhood" because she always wore a ragged hood over her matted black hair.

When the King died, the Queen was left with only her two daughters. But she did not grow to love Tatterhood any better, for the child was noisy and always up to mischief. Unlike her mother, Belinda loved Tatterhood dearly, and wherever her sister went she always followed.

One Christmas Eve, when the children were nearly grown, Belinda sat reading while Tatterhood charged about the palace on her goat, banging with her spoon and pretending she was battling a fierce dragon. Suddenly such a crashing and howling arose in the topmost gallery of the palace that even Tatterhood's racket was drowned out. Off she raced to find her mother and demand what was the matter.

"Go back to your play," sighed the Queen. "It has nothing to do with you." But Tatterhood would not cease her questioning until the Queen gave in and told her about the pack of witches who came every seven years to keep Christmas in the palace. No one had the courage to stop them, so great was their evil power.

"I'll drive them out!" said Tatterhood.

"No! No!" cried the Queen and begged her to leave the witches alone lest something dreadful happen.

"Do not be afraid, dear Mother," said Tatterhood as she headed off to do battle. "There is only one thing I require. You must promise to make sure that all the doors leading into the gallery are shut and locked. Not one must be forgotten!" The Queen promised to do exactly as Tatterhood ordered.

The gallery was teeming with witches. As Tatterhood entered, they leapt on her, pulling her hair and biting and scratching. But the brave girl swung her wooden spoon like a great club until the witches were flying before her like leaves in a whirlwind. Howling and screeching, they began to fly out through the windows.

At the very last moment, when nearly all the witches were gone, a door creaked open and in peeked Belinda. "Tatterhood," she began, "are you all — ?"

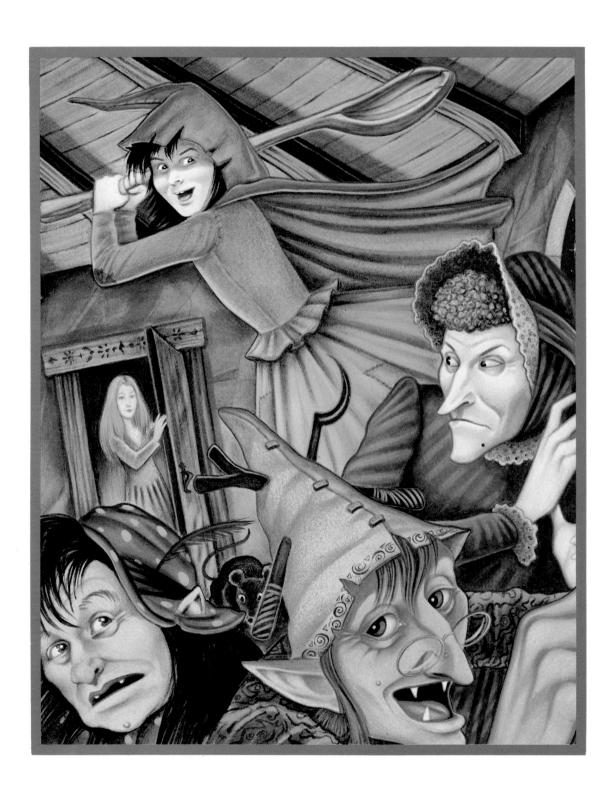

Before Tatterhood could say a word, the last witch caught sight of Belinda and rushed upon her. The hag snatched the child's head from her shoulders and put a calf's head in its place. Shrieking with laughter, she flew out through the window and disappeared into the night.

The Queen was horrified when Belinda came down from the gallery, and Tatterhood scolded her mother fiercely for not seeing that all the gallery doors were locked. All Belinda could say was, "Mooo, mooo, mooo..."

That night the Queen wept bitterly at the misfortune her carelessness had caused, and Tatterhood began to regret her harsh words. "Do not cry, dear Mother," she said. "I will set my sister free. I must have a ship in full trim, but I want no captain or crew. If we are to succeed, Belinda and I must set out on this voyage alone."

The ship was soon ready, a magnificent vessel with sails billowing like gossamer in the breeze. Riding her goat, and waving her wooden spoon, Tatterhood led her poor calf-headed sister on board.

The Queen was heartbroken at seeing her daughters leave. "Tatterhood," she cried, "can you forgive me for being so cruel to you all these years? I will die of grief if you and your sister do not come back."

"We will be back," said Tatterhood firmly, "and with husbands too!" With this strange prophecy she cast off the ropes and headed the ship out into the mysterious ocean.

Night and day Tatterhood steered the ship, never leaving the helm. After many long weeks she at last caught sight of Witches' Isle looming like a jagged tooth on the horizon. Under a dark and jutting cliff Tatterhood anchored the ship where it could not be seen.

From one lonely window in the witches' castle a light flickered. As Tatterhood drew near, she could see Belinda's lovely head swinging from the frame. Softly as a moon shadow she flitted from rock to rock until she was directly below the window. Inside the castle she could hear the witches at their revels.

Tatterhood took a deep breath, then quick as a frog's tongue leapt up to the window, snatched the head and raced away. A cry of alarm, dreadful and shrill, pierced the night. The witches, thick as bees, poured from the castle.

As they swarmed around her, screaming and tearing at her clothes, Tatterhood wielded her spoon like a mighty sword. At last the frenzied witches fell back and she raced to the ship with Belinda's head clasped in her arm.

Safe on deck, Tatterhood gently removed the calf's head and put her sister's own lovely head back in its place. "Now, my dearest Belinda," she announced, "the second half of our quest can begin!" And with a shout of triumph, she flung the calf's head at the witches who were screaming from the shore.

Week after week they sailed on, until one bright morning they sighted land. Soon the spires of a great city appeared in the distance.

As Tatterhood steered the ship into port, the Prince of the land caught sight of it from a high turret in the castle. Immediately he sent messengers to find out where it came from and who was the captain.

The messengers returned with a very strange story to tell. All they had seen was a ragamuffin girl riding a goat around the deck, laughing and waving a wooden spoon like someone possessed.

"Ahoy!" they had shouted. "Where are the captain and crew of this vessel?"

"I am the captain," Tatterhood had replied. "And I am the crew."

"What is your business here?"

"That is for your Prince to discover," Tatterhood had shouted back.

When the Prince heard this he was overcome with curiosity, and at dawn the next day he called his brother and hurried down to the shore to see the strange girl for himself.

But instead of Tatterhood, Belinda was at the rail. The moment the Prince set eyes on her, he fell hopelessly in love. "I have waited all my life for someone as lovely as you," he declared. "Please, will you marry me? If you will not be my bride I will spend the rest of my life in utter misery."

"I cannot be married," Belinda said, "until my dear sister also has a husband."

"For the sister of one so lovely," said the Prince, "a husband should be easy to find."

But just at that moment, Tatterhood clattered out on deck and the Prince's joy failed him. Striving to hide his disappointment, he announced, "I would be honoured if you both would join me in a great banquet at the castle the day after tomorrow."

"We will accept your invitation gladly, my Lord," Tatterhood replied with a grand flourish of her wooden spoon.

The next day, dozens of presents from the Prince arrived at the ship. There were dresses of satin and silk, chests filled with pearl necklaces, ruby rings and sapphire bracelets. There were combs of gold, dainty little slippers and Arabian perfumes of exquisite scent. Belinda ran to and fro, trying on one thing after another, posing and twisting in front of a mirror while Tatterhood looked on in amusement.

"Won't you at least take off your hood and brush your hair?" pleaded Belinda.

"Good heavens, no!" said Tatterhood. "I shall go as I am." And she would say no more.

At the castle, the Prince was pacing in a fever of anxiety. "The elder sister looks so awful that even a blind man would not want her," he groaned. "But if I cannot find her a husband, I can never marry the princess I love."

The Prince's younger brother, Galen, was first of all amused and then touched by his brother's distress. "My goodness, if it bothers you so much, I will escort her to the banquet myself. Who knows, I may even be able to find a husband for her and put you out of your misery."

When the day of the banquet arrived, welcome banners fluttered in the streets as the townspeople turned out to see the visitors. At the head of the procession rode the Prince and Belinda, both on fine white steeds. Next came Prince Galen riding a stallion with silver trappings. And beside him, mounted on her goat and proud as any lord, was Tatterhood. Behind them came scores of knights and courtiers dressed in splendid livery.

Galen could not take his eyes off Tatterhood, and at last he summoned up the courage to speak. "You must be very brave," he said shyly.

"Why do you say that?" asked Tatterhood. "Do you see me as brave?"

"Of course I do!" said Galen. "The town is buzzing with the news of how you foiled the witches. No one has ever dared set foot on Witches' Isle. I certainly wouldn't."

Tatterhood laughed. "As you see me, so I am. What else have you noticed?"

"Well," said Galen, still a little hesitantly, "I see that even though you could ride the finest horse in the kingdom, you prefer to ride a goat."

"Do you see a goat?" asked Tatterhood. In a flash her goat was transformed into a magnificent charger.

"What an amazing person you are!" exclaimed Galen. "I also see that you are carrying a wooden spoon, which I am sure has dented the head of many a witch."

"You see a spoon?" asked Tatterhood, and instantly it became the loveliest silver wand imaginable.

Prince Galen looked at Tatterhood for a long time. "I also notice that you are wearing an old ragged dress," he said slowly.

"Ragged dress?" answered Tatterhood, pretending to be surprised. As she spoke the dress became a beautiful gown that shimmered like woven beams of moonlight.

Now Prince Galen laughed out loud. "I see that you are wearing a tattered hood, no doubt to hide your lovely hair and beautiful face?"

"Of course!" laughed Tatterhood, and all at once the old hood fell away, revealing the face of a maiden more lovely than all the stars of heaven. "As you see me, so I am."

The crowd gasped at the spectacle and then broke into joyous cheering, as the Prince reached over and took Tatterhood's hand.

"I have seen enough," he said.

A month later there was another grand procession — a wedding procession. For their honeymoon, the two young couples set sail for the homeland of the brides, where there was a joyful reunion with the Queen — and yet another banquet. Tatterhood and Belinda both had lovely children of their own and they lived in great peace and contentment to the very end of their days.